Chad and Chen

CATHERINE MALASKI • LISA PERRETT

Chad had a chum.

It was Chen.

Chad had a chip.

It was such a
big chip.

Chen had a dot on
her chin.

It was a chip!

It was an inch.

Chad and
Chen chat.

Chad and Chen chop!

Chad and Chen
had such fun.

Chad	chin	chum
chat	chip	inch
Chen	chop	such

Decodable Words

an	fun	on
big	had	
dot	it	

High-Frequency Words

a	her
and	was